LEGEND OF THE LURE

BY JAKE MADDOX

illustrated by Sean Tiffany

text by Bob Temple

Librarian Reviewer
Chris Kreie
Media Specialist, Eden Prairie Schools, MN
MS in Information Media, St. Cloud State University, MN

Reading Consultant
Mary Evenson
Middle School Teacher, Edina Public Schools, MN
MA in Education University of Min

STONE ARCH BOOKS
www.stonearchbooks.com

Jake Maddox Books are published by Stone Arch Books,
A Capstone Imprint
151 Good Counsel Drive, P.O. Box 669
Mankato, Minnesota 56002
www.capstonepub.com

Library of Congress Cataloging-in-Publication Data
Maddox, Jake.
    Legend of the Lure / by Jake Maddox; illustrated by Sean Tiffany.
    p. cm. — (Impact Books. A Jake Maddox Sports Story)
    ISBN 978-1-4342-0783-8 (library binding)
    ISBN 978-1-4342-0879-8 (pbk.)
    [1. Fishing—Fiction.] I. Tiffany, Sean, ill. II. Title.
PZ7.M25643Le 2009
[Fic]—dc22   2008004293

Summary: Daniel has always heard stories about Big Larry, and when
his grandpa dies, he is determined to catch the big fish.

Art Director: Heather Kindseth
Graphic Designer: Kay Fraser

Printed in the United States of America in Stevens Point, Wisconsin.
082011
006341R

TABLE OF CONTENTS

CHAPTER 1

FISH STORIES

Daniel smiled as he leaned back in the boat. This was a great day.

He was right where he wanted to be, sitting in Grandpa Carl's fishing boat. They were out in the middle of Lake Werner. It was Daniel's favorite place to be.

He'd been there many times before. Every summer for almost all fifteen years of Daniel's life, Grandpa Carl had taken Daniel fishing any time he wanted.

Just about every Saturday morning, rain or shine, Grandpa Carl would be at the door. He'd wait for Daniel to come out. They'd hop in the truck. Then they'd drive to the dock. There, Daniel would help his grandpa get the boat into the water.

They'd spend most of the morning together on the lake. They'd catch as many fish as they could.

They hardly ever ended up keeping the fish they caught, though. "It's a lot more fun to catch 'em than it is to eat 'em," Grandpa Carl would say.

Then he'd unhook a fish and send it over the side. The fish could swim back to freedom.

Daniel loved everything about fishing. He wasn't sure what his favorite part was.

He loved feeling the tug of a fish at the end of the line. He loved putting bait on the hook. And he really loved battling with a big fish until he brought it into the boat.

The stories that Grandpa Carl told were almost as good as the real thing. And sometimes, they were better.

Grandpa's best stories were always about two things. First, he loved to tell Daniel all about the annual Lake Werner Fishing Tournament. He also loved to tell stories about Big Larry.

Big Larry was the name Grandpa Carl had given to the biggest fish he'd ever seen in the lake. He had many stories about having Big Larry on his line. In all the stories, the fish got away just as Grandpa was about to pull him into the boat.

"That fish is about as old as I am, I guess," Grandpa Carl always said. "We've had our share of battles over the years. Every time I see him, he's a little bit bigger than before. I think he's got me figured out now. Sometimes I see him swim up next to the boat. Seems like he's almost trying to say hello to an old friend."

With that, Grandpa would pull off his old fishing hat. "See this lure here?" he'd say. He would point to the lure hooked to the side of the hat.

There wasn't anything special about the lure. It didn't look like it was swimming in the water like some lures did, or anything like that.

It was just a small, orange, metal lure. But it was special to Daniel, because of the story that went with it.

"I used that lure the last time I hooked Big Larry," Grandpa would say. "Now, that's a story. Have I told you that one?"

Daniel always said no, even though he'd heard the story a thousand times. Then Grandpa Carl would start telling the story as if he'd never told it before.

Daniel didn't care that he already knew the story. He liked hearing it anyway. He loved the happy look on his grandfather's face as he told the story of hooking the giant fish.

"I fought him for more than an hour, and he still had fight in him," Grandpa always said. He'd smile and describe it all to Daniel.

The story ended the same way it always did.

At the last minute, Grandpa had been about to pull Big Larry into the boat. And just before he did, the fish spit the hook out.

Grandpa would say, "And that's when the fish hooked me, right in the cheek, just like I'd hooked him!"

Then Daniel's grandfather would point to the scar on his cheek for proof. And Daniel, just like always, would laugh at the story. Then he'd ask his grandpa to tell him another one.

[CHAPTER 2]

DANIEL'S PROMISE

Grandpa Carl loved to fish, and he loved the Lake Werner Fishing Tournament, too. He'd entered the event for more than forty years in a row, but he'd never won it. But every year, he was sure it was his turn.

"The tournament is this coming weekend," Grandpa Carl told Daniel as they fished. "One of these years, I'll pull Big Larry in. Then I'll be the champ. Now that would be something."

Later that morning, Grandpa let Daniel steer his prized boat toward shore.

Daniel said, "Grandpa, we've fished together for years. But I've never even seen Big Larry." He paused. He wasn't sure if his grandpa was just telling tall fishing tales, like he knew many fishermen did. "Why do you think that is?" Daniel asked.

Grandpa Carl chuckled. "Now, you aren't doubting your own grandpa, are you?" he asked, smiling. "Why, I saw Big Larry just a couple of months ago. I was out fishing one morning. You were at school. Sure enough, he swam right up next to the boat. Just like he was saying hello."

Daniel smiled. "One of these times, I want to be there when you're battling him," he said.

Then Grandpa's face really lit up. "Who knows?" he said. "Maybe you'll be the one to catch him. Now that would be something."

"That would be awesome," Daniel said.

Suddenly, Grandpa Carl frowned. "Danny boy, you've got to promise me one thing," he said. "If you ever do catch him, you have to let him go."

"Okay, Grandpa, I will," Daniel said. "We almost always let the fish we catch go anyway."

"Yes, but Big Larry is extra special," Grandpa Carl said. "A lot of people who fish this lake want to catch him. They'd like to mount him and hang him up on their walls."

Grandpa shook his head, looking angry.

Then he added, "Big Larry is not someone's trophy, and he's definitely not someone's dinner. He deserves to live out his final years here in Lake Werner."

Daniel could tell that his grandpa was serious. He was also pretty sure that Big Larry was real.

Grandpa Carl liked to tell jokes, and he was known to take a good story and make it a little better by adding some untrue details. But he would never get so serious over something that wasn't real.

Daniel carefully guided the boat up alongside the dock. Grandpa had taught him how to drive a boat.

Over the years, Grandpa Carl's eyesight had started to get worse. He didn't like to drive the boat anymore.

Daniel was happy to get the chance to drive the boat. He loved it.

They tied up the boat and walked up the dock. At a snack counter, they each grabbed a sandwich. Then they sat down to eat on the worn wooden benches.

"Grandpa, how will I know it's Big Larry if I catch him?" Daniel asked.

"Oh, you'll know," Grandpa Carl said with a laugh. "For one thing, he's huge! For another, Big Larry has a yellow stripe that goes halfway down his side. I'm telling you, he's one special fish. He's like an old friend to me."

After they finished eating, it was time to go home. But Daniel noticed that something was different about Grandpa Carl.

Usually, they would spend the ride home retelling the stories from their day of fishing. But today, Grandpa Carl didn't talk at all during the whole ride home.

Finally, when they arrived at Daniel's house, Grandpa Carl turned and looked at him. "Daniel, you have to make me that promise," he said. "Promise me you'll let Big Larry go if you catch him."

"I will, Grandpa," Daniel said. "I swear."

[CHAPTER 3]

GRANDPA CARL

That night, Daniel had to babysit his neighbor, Brian. He headed to Brian's house right after dinner.

Brian was only six years old. He really liked it when Daniel came to babysit.

They usually spent most of the night playing video games, wrestling, or watching sports on TV. Sometimes, Daniel would tell Brian about his fishing trips with Grandpa Carl.

Brian had never gone fishing in his life. He wasn't quite sure what he thought of stories about Big Larry and the fishing tournament.

The stories didn't mean much to Brian, but he thought they were interesting and exciting. He told Daniel that he wanted to go fishing too.

"One day, when you get older, maybe your parents will let me take you fishing," Daniel told Brian. "Now that would really be something."

"That would be awesome," Brian said.

Later that night, Daniel put Brian to bed by reading him one of his favorite books. It was after 11 o'clock when Brian finally fell asleep. Then Daniel headed back downstairs.

Daniel took a peek out of the window in Brian's living room. He looked through the trees at his own house, which was right next door.

Usually, his parents turned off their bedroom light at 10. But tonight, he noticed right away, his parents were both awake.

The lights were still on in the house. Daniel could see his dad walking around. It looked like he was talking on the phone.

Who could he be talking to at this time of night? Daniel thought.

Daniel brushed away his worry. It was probably no big deal.

He settled down in front of the TV to play some video games. He knew that would help him stay awake.

Finally, just after midnight, Brian's parents returned home. They paid Daniel and thanked him. Then he left.

When Daniel walked in the front door of his house, he started to worry again.

His parents were still awake. They were sitting in the living room, waiting for him to come home.

The fact that they were even awake was weird. The fact that they were sitting there, waiting for him, was really weird.

Then Daniel noticed that his parents' eyes were red and puffy.

"What's going on?" he asked, frowning.

"Daniel, we have to talk about your grandpa," said Daniel's dad. It seemed like he was fighting back tears.

"He was out for dinner with Grandma tonight, and he had a heart attack," Daniel's dad continued.

"Is he all right? Can we go see him?" Daniel asked quickly.

His dad lowered his head. He didn't say anything.

"Honey, no," Daniel's mom said. "Grandpa Carl died tonight. I'm so sorry."

Daniel didn't know what to say or do. He just stood there.

He felt sadness growing inside of him, but no tears came.

"But I was just fishing with him this morning," Daniel said. "And he was fine. He was telling stories, and talking about the next fishing tournament, and Big Larry, and—"

Then the reality hit Daniel hard. His body began to shake. He suddenly felt really cold.

His mom got up and hugged him. That's when Daniel started crying.

He couldn't believe what was happening. His grandpa was dead. Daniel felt like his own life was over, too.

CHAPTER 4

GRANDPA'S HAT

For the next few days, Daniel felt like he was in a fog.

He couldn't believe what was happening, and he just wanted to stop it. He felt like he was in a really long bad dream.

Hundreds of people came to Grandpa Carl's funeral. Daniel was glad that his grandpa had so many friends, but he still hated the funeral.

He didn't like seeing his grandpa's body in the front of the church. It really bothered him that Grandpa Carl had been dressed in a suit. For as long as Daniel had been alive, his grandfather had never worn a suit.

He knew that all the visitors meant well, but he didn't like hearing over and over how sorry people were. And they just kept saying things that bugged him.

"I know your grandpa was very special to you," they would say. "I'm sorry that he had to go. But he's in a better place."

A better place? Daniel thought angrily. *How could that be?*

Grandpa Carl's days had been spent either fishing or spending time with Grandma. Nothing could be better than that.

Finally, one person said, "Think of it this way. Up in heaven, your grandpa can probably fish any time he likes. I bet he's always making the big catch."

Then Daniel had heard enough. He ran out of the church. He sat quietly on the front steps of the church with his head in his hands.

After a few minutes, his grandma walked outside and sat down next to him.

"This stinks, doesn't it?" Daniel's grandma said.

"Yeah," Daniel said. "Grandpa would hate this day. If he were here right now, he'd pull me aside and say, 'Hey kid, let's get out of here and go fishing.'"

Grandma laughed. "You're right about that!" she said.

Then she was quiet for a few moments. "Danny, none of us were ready for this," she said finally. "We just have to keep going. We have to do the best we can."

"Yeah, I know," Daniel said.

Grandma smiled at him. "Well, I have something for you," she said. "I know your grandpa wanted you to have this."

She pulled Grandpa's old fishing hat out of her purse and handed it to Daniel.

"You two didn't always catch much, but whenever your grandfather came home from a fishing trip with you, he was wearing a smile on his face," Grandma said. "When you come over tomorrow, you can go through Grandpa's fishing stuff. You can take whatever you want. Those things all belong to you now."

Daniel's hands shook a little as he clutched the hat. He looked closely at the lure that Grandpa Carl said he had used to hook Big Larry. That's when he noticed the tiny letters and numbers scratched into the side of the lure.

BL 6-12-1996.

Grandpa Carl must have put the date there after his big battle with the mighty fish. The date — June 12, 1996 — must have been when the battle happened. And the "BL," well, that stood for "Big Larry."

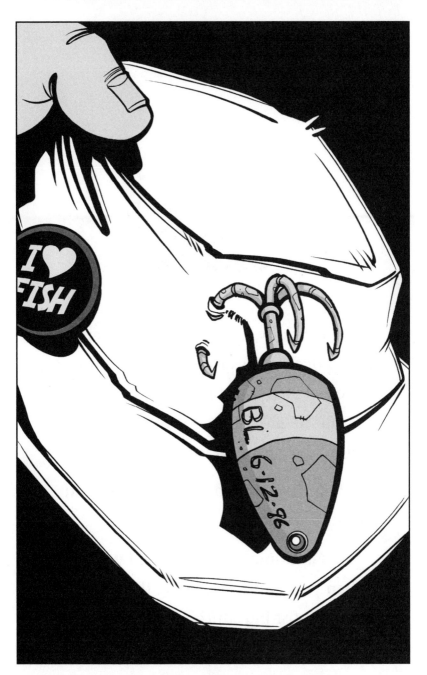

[CHAPTER 5]

A PRIZED CATCH

The next day, Daniel and his parents headed over to his grandparents' house. He was excited to get his grandpa's fishing gear, but he also felt sad that his grandpa wouldn't be with him to use it.

When they arrived, Daniel's grandma gave him a hug.

"Hi, Grandma," he said. "Did you mean it when you said I could look through Grandpa's fishing stuff?"

His grandma smiled. "Of course, honey. Most of your grandpa's fishing gear was in the garage," she said. "But he had a lot of stuff that he kept down in the basement, too. Some of the older stuff is down there. I don't know if you want it or not, but it wouldn't hurt to look."

"I'd like to look," Daniel said. "Can you show me?"

Grandma led him down to a dark part of the basement. Daniel had spent a lot of time playing down there, but he'd never gone into the dirty, dusty corner where Grandpa's workbench was.

Grandma turned on a light over the workbench. "Well, here it is, Daniel," she said. "I don't know what's in those boxes, but you're welcome to look. Take anything you want."

Daniel stood and looked around. On the wall in front of him was a rack full of fishing poles. The boxes under the workbench were full of lures and other fishing gear.

He looked for a while, but Daniel didn't want anything he found down in the basement. He wanted to take the gear that Grandpa Carl had used when they fished together. Most of that stuff was in the garage. Daniel decided to go back upstairs.

He reached for the light. But then he noticed a picture on the wall behind the workbench. It was dusty, but Daniel recognized the man in the picture right away. It was Grandpa Carl.

In the picture, Grandpa was standing proudly on a dock. He was holding up a prized catch.

Wow, that's a big fish, Daniel thought. He paused for a second and studied the photo. He wiped the dust off with his shirt. Then he looked at the picture again. The more closely he looked, the more he couldn't believe what he was seeing.

His grandpa was proudly holding a giant fish. And that giant fish had a yellow stripe that went halfway down its side.

It was Big Larry.

CHAPTER 6

BIG LARRY LANDED?

Daniel clutched the picture. He ran upstairs. His parents and grandma were sitting at the kitchen table, drinking coffee and talking.

"Grandma! Do you know anything about this picture?" Daniel yelled.

Grandma peered at the picture. "Oh yes. Your grandpa's had that picture on his workbench for years," she said. "That was quite a fish."

Daniel wanted to hear more. "Do you know when this was taken?" he asked. "And where? And who took it?"

"Hold on," Grandma said. "Take a look at the back of the photo. Your grandpa always wrote on the back of them."

Daniel quickly flipped the picture over. In his grandpa's handwriting, it said: "Big Larry Landed! 6/12/96."

He looked at the photo again, staring closely at his grandpa's face. There, on Grandpa's right cheek, was the familiar scar. But that didn't make sense.

Grandpa had always said he got that scar fighting with Big Larry. If that was true, it should have been bleeding in this picture. It shouldn't have already become a scar.

Now Daniel felt even more confused. "Grandma, you know the scar on Grandpa's cheek?" he asked.

"You mean the one he got in the war, honey?" she replied. "What about it?"

"The war?" Daniel mumbled. "Oh. Never mind."

"You know, I never understood why he didn't keep the fish in that picture," Daniel's grandma continued. "That was the biggest fish he ever caught. By the looks of it, I'd say it was one of the biggest in the state. It would have looked good on the wall. Your grandpa threw it back."

Daniel's dad smiled. "Probably would have tasted good, too," he said.

"I know why," Daniel muttered.

The grownups all stared at him.

Daniel took a breath. Then he explained, "Grandpa loved to fish. He probably had a great time catching that fish. And he probably wanted to do it again. That's why he let it go."

Daniel's grandma said, "Knowing your grandpa, he probably put that fish back so that someone else could have the same fun he had that day."

She smiled. Then she added, "Maybe someone like you."

[CHAPTER 7]

THE TOURNAMENT

It didn't take long before Daniel had decided to compete in the annual Lake Werner Fishing Tournament.

When they heard he wanted to enter, the tournament organizers allowed him to take his grandpa's spot in the tournament. Daniel planned to use his grandpa's boat and all of his equipment. In fact, Daniel decided, he would try to catch Big Larry during the tournament.

He would spend the two days thinking about his grandfather. Maybe that would help him stop feeling so sad.

The tournament was a two-day event. Anglers could get on the water at 7 o'clock in the morning each day, and they had to be off the water by 3 o'clock in the afternoon.

It was a catch-and-release tournament. That meant that anglers had to keep any fish they caught alive. They'd keep the fish in special holders on their boats.

At the end of each day, the fish would be weighed. Then the anglers would release the fish back into the lake. Whichever angler caught the most weight in fish over the two days would be the winner of the tournament.

On the first day of the tournament, Daniel was on the water bright and early. He caught a couple of small fish right away, but that was it.

He didn't catch anything at all after noon. That meant he had a lot of time to think.

He moved the boat expertly around the lake, looking for fishing spots. He kept hoping that Big Larry would show up next to the boat, just as Grandpa Carl had said he would. At least then Daniel would see the fish for himself.

He knew one thing for sure. Big Larry was real. His grandpa had even caught him once.

But that was several years ago. What if Big Larry was dead?

However, Daniel remembered, Grandpa Carl had made Daniel promise that if he caught Big Larry, he'd release him. So Grandpa must have believed that Big Larry was still alive.

It was almost 3 p.m. Time to get ready to leave the lake. Daniel began to pack up his gear. Just as he was about to start the boat's motor, he felt something hit the side of the boat. Quickly, he leaned over the boat's edge and peered into the water.

Nothing.

Feeling disappointed, he started up the boat and headed for shore.

The first day of the tournament had not gone like he imagined it would. Not at all.

CHAPTER 8

FRESH FISH!

That night, Brian's parents asked him to babysit again while they went to a movie. Daniel and Brian decided to go to the grocery store to get something to eat for dinner.

The store was only a couple of blocks away, so it was a short walk. At the store, they sped through the chips and salsa section. Daniel didn't even let Brian stop and look at the candy bars.

Daniel was in a hurry. He wanted to get Brian home and fed as fast as possible. Then he'd be able to make a plan for the next day.

As they walked through the meat section, Brian pulled away from Daniel. "Hey!" he yelled. "Look at that huge fish! It's like a giant monster fish or something!"

Daniel's eyes shot over to the fresh fish case. There, packed in ice, was the biggest fish he had ever seen. Next to it was a sign that read, "FRESH FISH! Pulled straight from Lake Werner!"

Daniel couldn't believe it. Slowly, he stepped closer to the chilly case. The fish was much bigger than the one in the picture in his grandpa's house. But running halfway down the side of the fish's body was a yellow stripe.

CHAPTER 9

NOT A TROPHY

Daniel stared at the huge fish. A chill ran up his spine.

He suddenly felt really sad. It was almost like his grandpa had died again. Daniel knew it was a strange way to feel, but he couldn't help it.

"I'm sorry, Larry," Daniel mumbled to the fish.

"What?" Brian asked. "What did you just say, Daniel?"

"Oh, nothing," Daniel said. "Never mind. Let's just go find the aisle that has the macaroni and cheese."

Daniel's heart thumped as he and Brian picked out their dinners. As they were about to check out, Daniel stopped. "Hang on," he said to Brian. "There's one more thing we need."

Daniel led Brian back to the fish case. The butcher behind the counter asked, "Can I help you?"

Daniel pointed at the huge fish and said, "I'll take that one."

"The whole thing?" the butcher asked, frowning.

Daniel nodded.

The butcher shrugged. "All right, kid," he said. "Whatever you say."

A few minutes later, Daniel and Brian were on their way back to Brian's. They were carrying the huge fish between them.

"Daniel, are we going to eat this fish?" Brian asked.

Daniel didn't reply right away. He thought about what Grandpa Carl had said. "Larry is not someone's trophy, and he's definitely not someone's dinner."

"No," Daniel told Brian. "We can't eat him. And I'm going to make sure no one does."

[CHAPTER 10]

SET THE FISH FREE

The next morning, Daniel knew what he had to do. He headed back out to Lake Werner for the second day of the fishing tournament.

His plan was pretty simple. He'd take the boat out into the middle of the lake. Then he would set the big fish free.

Daniel knew that the fish was already dead. It wasn't like he was really letting the fish escape back into the wild.

However, he also knew that his grandpa would have wanted the fish to rest in the lake. Grandpa Carl would have hated the idea of the big fish being sold in a grocery store. He really would've hated knowing that Big Larry was on someone's plate.

When he arrived at Lake Werner, Daniel put his grandpa's hat on. Then he guided the boat out to the spot where his grandpa had caught Big Larry.

When he reached the spot, he knew it was time to throw back the big fish. Before he did anything, though, Daniel wanted to bait his line.

He dug through his fishing gear, but somehow, there wasn't a lure to be found. He had lots of fishing line, and some spare hooks, but that was it.

No lures. Not even any broken ones.

Then Daniel realized that he had a spare. He reached up to his head and took off his grandpa's hat.

Daniel baited his line with the lure from his grandpa's hat. Then he carefully sent the line out and started pulling it in.

After all, he was still in a fishing tournament. And, he knew, that lure had caught a big fish before.

Then he reached into his bag and pulled out the frozen fish. He carefully started to unwrap it.

Just then, his fishing pole smacked against the side of the boat. The pole was climbing up the side of the boat, pulled by something on the other end.

Something had been hooked!

The pole was close to falling into the water when Daniel grabbed it. He held the pole and started to pull in the line. But the tug from whatever was on the other end was too strong.

Daniel remembered his grandpa's story about the day he caught Big Larry.

"I let him tire himself out," Grandpa had said. "And that's when I started to pull him in. But he still had a lot of fight left."

Daniel knew his grandpa's advice was the way to go. He let the fish fight so that it would get tired.

After about 20 minutes, Daniel was able to start to pull the strong fish in. He glanced over his shoulder at the frozen pack in the boat. The big, dead fish was still there.

Daniel kept battling with the fish in the lake. Finally, he was able to pull the fish up next to the boat. He grabbed his net and waited.

Then the fish showed itself in the dark water. Daniel thought it was looking him right in the eye. It was the biggest fish Daniel had ever seen. It was even bigger than the one he'd bought at the store.

With one quick motion, Daniel scooped the fish with his net. He carefully unhooked it from the line. Then he dropped it into a tank of water. It was almost too big to fit.

As he dropped the fish, Daniel noticed something amazing. There was a yellow stripe that ran halfway down the fish's side!

Daniel compared the picture of his grandpa with Big Larry to the fish.

It was him! It was definitely Big Larry. The fish from the grocery store may have been the same kind as Big Larry, but it wasn't him.

Instantly, Daniel rushed to shore to get the huge fish weighed.

The tournament director peered into Daniel's boat.

He yelled, "Wow, kid! You caught Big Larry! Anglers around here have been trying to catch him for years. How did you do it?"

Daniel smiled. "My grandpa helped," he said.

[CHAPTER 11]

LETTING LARRY GO

Later that day, Daniel became his family's first winner of the Lake Werner Fishing Tournament. After he'd had his picture taken with Big Larry, Daniel headed quietly back out on the lake.

In the middle of the lake, he turned off his boat's motor.

First, he threw the frozen fish into the water. It didn't deserve to be anyone's dinner either.

Then Daniel grabbed the giant, living fish. He said goodbye to Big Larry and eased him into the lake.

The huge fish paused. He turned around. He seemed to look at Daniel one more time.

Then, with a strong swish of his powerful tail, Big Larry swam away.

ABOUT THE AUTHOR

Bob Temple lives in Rosemount, Minnesota, with his wife and three children. He has written more than thirty books for children. Over the years, he has coached more than twenty kids' soccer, basketball, and baseball teams. He also loves visiting classrooms to talk about his writing.

ABOUT THE ILLUSTRATOR

When Sean Tiffany was growing up, he lived on a small island off the coast of Maine. Every day, from sixth grade until he graduated from high school, he had to take a boat to get to school. When Sean isn't working on his art, he works on a multimedia project called "OilCan Drive," which combines music and art. He has a pet cactus named Jim.

GLOSSARY

angler (AYNG-lur)—someone who fishes

annual (AN-yoo-uhl)—something that happens once every year

bait (BATE)—food used to attract a fish so that it can be caught

dock (DOK)—a structure that sticks out into the water, from which people get in or out of boats

familiar (fuh-MIL-yur)—well-known or easily recognized

line (LINE)—a length of thin cord attached to a fishing rod

lure (LOOR)—an artificial bait made of plastic or metal, which looks like food to a fish. When the fish tries to eat the lure, it is caught.

mount (MOUNT)—to set in place for display

tournament (TUR-nuh-muhnt)—a contest in which a number of people try to win the top prize

trophy (TROH-fee)—a prize or award

GET STARTED FISHING!

Serious anglers can spend thousands of dollars on special fishing rods, different kinds of fishing line, all kinds of other equipment, plus a boat. But you don't really need all of that to have fun fishing. All you need is a lake or stream that has fish in it, some basic equipment, and lots of patience!

Here's what you need to get started.

Equipment: You will need a rod and reel with some fishing line. You will also need some hooks and sinkers. You can also get some bobbers. These little floaters sit on top of the water, and they bounce up and down when the fish are nibbling. When the bobber disappears underwater, you know you've caught something!

Lures: The best lures for kids to use are good old-fashioned worms! You can dig them up yourself or buy them from a bait store. You can also get some minnows to use as bait if you like. If you don't want to use anything alive for bait, you can get some rubber worms or other plastic or metal lures.

Patience: Fishing takes time and lots and lots of patience. You need to be able to sit still for a while, or you'll scare the fish away!

What you don't need:

A boat: Fishing in a boat is fun, but it's just as much fun to fish off a dock or from the shore of a lake. That way, if you get bored, you can always stop and take some breaks!

DISCUSSION QUESTIONS

1. Why did Grandpa Carl and Daniel want to throw Big Larry back into the water after they caught him?

2. Grandpa Carl told Daniel that his scar was from a battle with Big Larry, but Grandma told Daniel that it was from the war. Why did Grandpa Carl make up a story about his scar?

3. If the big fish that Daniel caught was Big Larry, can you explain the smaller fish he found at the grocery store?

○WRITING PROMPTS○

1. Losing a loved one is difficult for anyone to handle. Have you ever had someone that you loved die? How did it make you feel?

2. Write a few paragraphs about one of your grandparents, living or dead. Include as many details as you can.

3. What's your favorite hobby or recreational activity? Write about what you like to do, why you like it, and how you share your interest with other people.

OTHER BOOKS

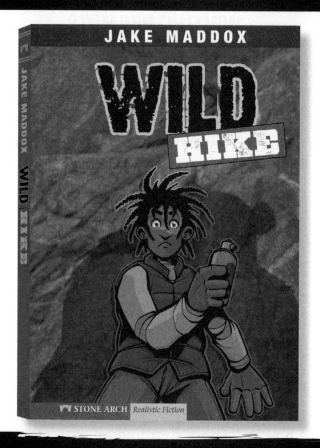

JAKE MADDOX

WILD HIKE

STONE ARCH *Realistic Fiction*

Nick has always loved camping, but his cousins don't listen to his warnings about campfires and bears, and they make fun of everything Nick does. When Devin finds himself in real danger, can Nick save him in time?

BY JAKE MADDOX

JAKE MADDOX

FREE CLIMB

JAKE MADDOX

FREE CLIMB

STONE ARCH *Realistic Fiction*

When a police officer offers to bring Amir to a climbing wall outside of the city, Amir is thrilled. He meets William, who also loves climbing. But William doesn't want to learn the right way to climb, and before long, he is in serious danger.

⚬INTERNET SITES ⚬

Do you want to know more about subjects related to this book? Or are you interested in learning about other topics? Then check out FactHound, a fun, easy way to find Internet sites.

Our investigative staff has already sniffed out great sites for you!

Here's how to use FactHound:

1. Visit *www.facthound.com*

2. Select your grade level.

3. To learn more about subjects related to this book, type in the book's ISBN number: **9781434207838**.

4. Click the **Fetch It** button.

FactHound will fetch the best Internet sites for you!